Kitty Tales™

The First Adventures of Nerma and Blueberry

by Ariana B. Farina

Illustrations by
Sunny Duran

Ariana Farina Consulting, LLC
2020

Book design Sunny Duran

Editor Catherine Nichols

First paperback edition November 2020

ISBN 978-1-7360033-1-2

Contents

Dedicated to my loving family.
I love you.

Chapter 1

NERMA AND HER CHRISTMAS BAGS

There once was a kitty named Nerma with fancy-looking black-and-white fur. She lived with her human family: Mom, Dad, and little Toby.

Other kitties would ask her why she was always dressed so fancy. She would respond, "Because you never know where you will wind up,

daaahhhling!"

It was almost Christmas time.
Nerma's mom and dad had been out
shopping all day. It was late.
Nerma wondered if they would ever
come home! Finally, Mom and Dad
returned home. Nerma had never seen
so many Christmas shopping bags
before. She saw striped bags, shiny
bags, glittery bags, and even a
wonderful polka-dotted bag. Nerma
loves polka dots.

"Ooooh! I want that polka-dotted
bag!" Nerma thought.

Nerma was excited because shopping bags contain fancy magical kitty parties that only kitties can see. Going to these parties was Nerma's extra-super-duper-favorite thing ever. There was the **Purrr-fect Party**, the **Fur Ball**, and the **Catwalk Fashion Show**.

But her favorite are Christmas parties!

"Oh, what lovely Christmas party will I get to go to this year?" Nerma thought. Nerma pranced around Mom. She was practicing her dance moves for the Christmas party.

Last year after shopping, Mom gave Nerma the most wonderful bag. But today Mom did not give any of the bags to Nerma. Mom put all of the bags into the closet. How would she go to a Christmas party now?

Mom saw that Nerma was sad and said, "I'm sorry, Nerma. I must hide these presents until I wrap them for Christmas. But here, I can give you this one."

Mom reached into a large bag. She pulled out a bag and gave it to Nerma.

The bag was tiny! Nerma put her head inside. That was all that would fit.

Inside the bag Nerma saw a surprise! It was not a party for cats. The bag was much too small to be a party for cats. It was a party for mice! Nerma saw mice dancing, singing Christmas carols, eating cheese, and being merry.

Nerma's huge cat head poking into the party scared the mice.

"Eeek! A cat!" yelled one of the mice.

"Whoops! Sorry! Wrong party," said Nerma.

She pulled her head out of the bag. "I guess a bag has to be larger to be a cat party," she thought.

Poor Nerma. She would not be going to a Christmas party that night after all. She was just too big for the mouse party! But Nerma still had hope. Christmas was only three days away. There was still time for Mom and Dad to give her the bags for Christmas.

The next day, Mom said, "Nerma, come help us decorate the tree."

But Nerma was too busy getting ready for the Christmas bag party. She tried on different bows to see which suited her best. Nerma decided red was her perfect color. She even made herself earrings out of Christmas tree ornaments. Nerma wanted to look just right for the party.

Finally, Christmas Eve arrived. Mom took all of the shopping bags into the den to wrap presents.

Dad said to Toby, "Mom is wrapping up all of her gifts. She will have them ready to give to you tomorrow along with Santa's gifts!"

Dad asked Mom, "Do you want me to throw these bags out when you are donc?"

Nerma's eyes grew wide with fear.
"NO, NO, NO! I need those!" thought
Nerma.

Mom started to say something to
Dad. But then, Mom closed the door to
the den. Nerma was on the other side.
Nerma put her ear to the door.

She wanted to
know Mom's
answer, but
she could not
hear one word.
Oh no! Did
Mom tell Dad
not to throw
the bags away?

Nerma was pretty sure that's what
Mom would have said. Well, she was
almost sure... Nerma decided she was
not going to worry about it.

Nerma could not sleep very well
that night. She tossed and turned in her
sleep. She was too excited for
Christmas morning.

At 6:00 a.m. sharp, Nerma woke up. She and Toby pounced on Mom and Dad's heads to wake them up. Nerma knew Toby wanted to see her presents, but Nerma wanted to see her bags. Head pouncing worked very well. Mom and Dad both sprung awake looking very surprised.

Soon everyone ran downstairs to enjoy Christmas. Nerma ran round and round the Christmas tree. She did not see any of the bags. Nerma ran into the den—no bags there either! Oh no, did Mom throw them all away? Nerma was soooooo sad.

Nerma slowly walked back into the living room to join her family. They were opening presents and looked quite merry.

"Nerma! You have presents under the tree, too," said Toby. Toby pulled out a small gift and read the tag.

To Nerma, with love, your loving human family.

WOW! Nerma did not expect this! Toby helped open the present.

Inside were cat treats! Toby fed Nerma
a cat treat. Dad tossed Nerma a new
toy mouse. Nerma happily chased
after it.

More and more presents were opened. Wrapping paper collected on the floor. Oh my! It was like a fort. Nerma pounced on the paper. She jumped in and out.

Her family giggled at this. All the pouncing made Nerma tired. She plopped down next to Toby. Toby petted Nerma, who purred happily.

Mom whispered in Nerma's ear, "We love you, Nerma."

Nerma thought, "I love you too! What a lovely party right here in my own home with my own family!"

It was so much fun! Nerma felt so loved. She had almost forgotten all about her bag party.

"We have one last gift for you, Nerma," said Dad. He pulled out the giant polka-dotted bag from the closet and placed it in front of Nerma. Mom and Dad hadn't forgotten about her bag after all!

Nerma peeked inside. It was filled with the best kitty party Nerma had ever seen—a Christmas Party! When Nerma entered, she was greeted by lovely kitties. The kitties were dressed in the **fanciest** of kitty winter clothing. One kitty handed a cup of warm milk to Nerma. The party was decorated with Christmas trees for kitties to climb, bells to jingle, and Christmas stockings for kitties to bat at.

Nerma said, "Thank you, my lovely kitty friends. You are too kind. This is the loveliest kitty party I have ever seen. Alas, I will have to join you later. My family is already giving me the most wonderful party a kitty could hope for."

As Nerma exited the bag, she was greeted by Toby. Toby petted and cuddled her. Nerma spent that evening with her family. It was the best party ever! And Toby even gave her the best piece of turkey from Christmas dinner. Yum!

chapter 2

NERMA AND HER NEW SHOES

You know that Nerma loves to attend **fancy** kitty parties. What you might not guess about Nerma is that she also loves **stinky** shoes. For Nerma, the stinkier the better.

You see, when Nerma was a kitten, her human parents put an old stinky sock in her cat bed. They wanted Nerma to get used to their human smell. Since that day, Nerma has loved **stinky** feet smell.

Yes, Nerma loved the stinky smell, but she also longed for her very own pair of shoes to wear. Sadly, shoes don't come in kitty sizes. Nerma tried on Mom's shoes once, but they were much too big.

Nerma tried on Toby's shoes too, but they were still too big. What was a fancy kitty like Nerma to do?

Well, Toby's dolly Darla had the most beautiful red satin shoes Nerma had ever seen. They were just Nerma's size. Nerma had asked Toby to borrow Darla's shoes by softly tugging on them.

"No, Nerma, those aren't yours," scolded Toby.

Nerma knew that Toby did not like to share things. Toby always kept Darla under her arm, so it was very hard for Nerma to get her paws in those shoes. But Nerma had a plan...

Toby took a nap
at 3:00 pm
every day.
This would be
the perfect time

for Nerma to grab Darla's shoes!
Nerma needed the shoes for a fancy
kitty party that very evening.

As it neared naptime, Nerma
followed Toby around.

"Oh, Nerma, you must love me so much to follow me around," said Toby.

"I do love you, Toby, but I also want those lovely shoes," Nerma thought.

It seemed like it was taking Toby forever to get tired.

"Why isn't she lying down? Why, why not?" pouted Nerma.

45

In fact, all of this running around made Nerma tired herself.

"Must keep my eyes open; must keep an eye out for Toby falling asleep… must… must… zzzzz…"

Nerma went **KERPLOP**. She fell into a cat nap!

A short time later, Nerma awoke.

"Oh, no, where is Toby?" she thought.

Toby was asleep on the couch.

"Phew, there she is," thought Nerma.

The doll was under Toby's arm. Only one foot was sticking out. Nerma gripped the lovely red shoe with her teeth and pulled it off Darla's foot. That was easy, but now for the hard part.

Nerma needed Toby to roll over and expose Darla's other foot.

"Hmmm, what to do, what to do," thought Nerma.

Then it came to her—Nerma flicked her whiskers in front of Toby's nose. This made Toby roll over as she itched her nose. After all, kitty whiskers are very tickly. Nerma quickly removed Darla's other shoe.

Just then, Toby rolled over again.

This time she rolled right on Nerma's tail, trapping it! Nerma held Darla's shoes tightly in her mouth.

"Oh no! Things are not going well," Nerma thought, panicking.

Nerma tried to free herself. She pulled on her tail. No luck.

"I know. I'll just put my whiskers near her nose again," thought Nerma.

She tried this, but this time Toby did not roll over. There was only one last thing to do. Nerma let out a huge, **"REEEEEEOOOOOOW!"**

Toby popped awake, and Nerma ran off with the shoes in her mouth.

Oh wow! Nerma's first pair of shoes! Nerma carefully pulled one onto her paw. Just then, Toby walked in.

"What are you doing with Darla's shoes? Those aren't yours!" Toby yelled.

Nerma had been caught red pawed. She felt ashamed and hung her head low. Nerma knew she should not have taken the shoes.

Nerma began to remove the shoe to give back to Toby. She knew giving them back to Toby was the right thing to do.

But Toby was looking at the red shoe on Nerma's paw. "You know what? Those shoes do look pretty good on you, Nerma," said Toby with a smile.

Nerma looked up, surprised by Toby's words.

"If sharing makes you happy, then maybe I like sharing after all," said Toby. "Nerma, it's okay if you borrow Darla's shoes, as long as you promise to return them."

Nerma happily agreed by blinking
her eyes. Toby helped Nerma into the
other shoe. Nerma looked wonderful,
just **MARVELOUS!**

That night at the kitty party, Nerma was the talk of the town. No one had ever seen such beautiful shoes on such a **fancy**-looking kitty before. The shoes were so lovely that Nerma didn't seem to mind that they weren't **stinky**.

Chapter 3

BLUEBERRY iS GOOD AT COUNTiNG

...22,23,24

You know that Nerma is a very **fancy** kitty who loves fancy parties. But did you know that Nerma is also a very clever kitty? She is full of exciting facts. For example, did you know you can use your claws to climb up the clothing in a closet?

Or that you can use a blanket to slide
across a smooth floor?

Nerma had never met a kitty as clever
as she.

Then, one magical day, her family adopted a kitten named Blueberry.

"This is your brother, Blueberry," Mom said to Nerma. "He is a polydactyl kitty. This means he is very special because he has extra toes."

Blueberry had a cream-colored body, brown feet, and big blue eyes. Nerma scampered around Blueberry to greet him. She sniffed him and watched him closely. This is the polite thing to do when you meet another cat.

"Hello, I'm Nerma. I'm your sister. I see you have a lot of toes, which is pretty neat. Toby's dolls have lots of shoes. Would you like me to find you a pair to wear?" asked Nerma.

Blueberry was silent. He did not even sniff Nerma. Sniffing Nerma would have been the polite kitty-like thing to do.

Nerma did not see that Blueberry was a bit scared in his new home. Blueberry just hid his head.

"What's wrong? Cat got your tongue? Ha! See the joke I made there? Ha-ha," laughed Nerma.

"I'm kind of sh-sh-shy, and this apartment looks sooooo b-b-big," said Blueberry softly.

Nerma was not used to soft-spoken kitties. All of her friends liked to talk a lot. Nerma wasn't sure what to say.

"Oh…," said Nerma.

Nerma wondered how she could have any fun with such a shy kitty.

Toby picked up Blueberry, and he shivered a little bit.

"It's okay, Blueberry. I'll put you in your kitty bed," said Toby. Blueberry looked up at Toby with big scared eyes. Toby petted Blueberry to comfort him.

Each day, Nerma greeted Blueberry good morning. She tried many ways to talk and play with Blueberry. She showed him her kitty dance moves. She told him about fancy parties.

She even gave him a cat toy.

He still would not move or talk. Nerma
had almost given up. Then one day…

She was lying near Blueberry and cleaning each of her cat toes. As she cleaned them, she counted her toes to make sure she got every single one.

"one, two, three," counted Nerma, all the way up to **18**.

This was the highest number she had ever heard a cat count because most cats have **18** toes.

"There! All done cleaning," Nerma thought. She was very pleased with herself.

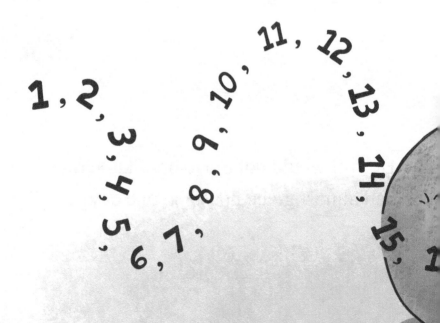

"19,20,21,22,23,24" said Blueberry as he cleaned his toes.

This surprised Nerma! She quickly lifted her head to look at Blueberry. He had two extra toes on each front paw and one extra toe on each back paw. Blueberry had **24** toes. This was six more toes!

"**WOW!** That was amazing! You might be the best kitty counter ever!" exclaimed Nerma.

Blueberry smiled. This made Nerma smile.

"You must come with me to the kitty talent show tonight. You can count all of your toes," said Nerma.

Blueberry gasped and hid his head once again.

"Oh, no! What's wrong?" asked a surprised Nerma.

"They will laugh at my feet. You said it yourself. I should wear shoes to cover them up," replied a sad Blueberry.

"Oh no, all the kitties will think your feet are great! I like shoes.

I thought you might like them too, but your paws are lovely without them," said Nerma.

She gave Blueberry a loving lick on his front paw.

"Really?" asked Blueberry.

"Really, really," replied Nerma.

Nerma found Blueberry some shoes to wear to the show. It was a pair from one of Toby's bigger dolls to fit Blueberry's larger paws. They were even blue to match his name!

That night, Nerma took Blueberry to the talent show. The two kitties watched the other kitties perform. One juggled some mice while the mice sang songs. One kitty gave tips on how much grass you could eat before barfing it up. Another kitty gave himself a full tongue bath in five seconds flat. These were clearly some very talented kitties. Seeing them made Blueberry feel even more shy.

Finally, it was Blueberry's turn. Nerma lightly pushed him onto the stage. Blueberry froze in stage fright. He covered his eyes with his paws.

"Let's give him some kitty help!" cheered Nerma.

The kitties nuzzled him. One even licked him on the nose. That surprised Blueberry. He giggled and uncovered his eyes.

Slowly he removed each shoe. He looked down at his feet and began to count, **"one, two, three"**

He got to **18** and kept going. The kitties at the talent show gasped.

"22,23,24!" finished Blueberry.

He looked up at the amazed kitties standing before him. All of the kitties clapped and cheered. Blueberry smiled a big toothy grin. Nerma smiled back at him.

Blueberry won first place at the talent show. The judge pinned a big blue ribbon on him. Not one single kitty laughed at his extra toes because they are quite wonderful after all.

Nerma and Blueberry returned home after the talent show. Nerma snuggled up to Blueberry. She said softly, "I am so proud of you. I am happy you are my new brother."

Blueberry grinned again and said, "I am glad you are my sister. Thank you for encouraging me. We are going to have some wonderful adventures together."

Then the two newfound friends drifted off to sleep. They dreamed happy dreams of adventures yet to come.

the Author's Tale

Ariana B. Farina has always loved cats. As a child, after a long day at school she loved to read funny and whimsical stories about animals. As an adult, she decided to combine these interests to write books for both children and parents to enjoy. Kitty Tales: The Book Series is inspired by her own two pet cats. You can enjoy photos of her real-life adorable kitties on Instagram @ kitty_tales_the_book_series.

Made in United States
Cleveland, OH
20 March 2025

15339118R00049